King Solomon and the Bee

King Solomon and the Bee

adapted by Dalia Hardof Renberg ✥ illustrated by Ruth Heller

Crocodile Books, USA

For Rennie, Dan, and Gil
—DHR

For King Solomon—
Stevie Graham
and the queen of Sheba—
Judy Sokoloff
—RH

This edition first published in the USA by

CROCODILE BOOKS
An imprint of Interlink Publishing Group, Inc.
46 Crosby Street, Northampton, Massachusetts 01060
www.interlinkbooks.com

Text copyright © Dalia Hardof Renberg, 1994, 2010
Illustrations copyright © Ruth M. Heller Trust, 1994
Illustrations copyright © Paul Heller and Philip Heller, 2010
Originally published in hardback by HarperCollins Publishers

Libary of Congress Cataloging-in-Publication Data
Renberg, Dalia Hardof.
King Solomon and the bee / adapted by Dalia Hardof Renberg ; illustrated by Ruth Heller.
p.   cm.
Summary: A retelling of the traditional tale about a bee that repays King Solomon's mercy
by helping him solve the Queen of Sheba's riddle.
ISBN 978-1-56656-815-9 (pbk.)—ISBN 0-06-022899-7.—ISBN 0-06-022902-0 (lib. bdg.)
1. Solomon, King of Israel—Legends. [I. Solomon, King of Israel. 2. Folklore, Jewish.] I. Heller, Ruth, date, ill.
II. Title.
PZ8.I.R2775Ki 1994   92-30411   398.22'095694—dc20 CIP
[E] AC

Typography by Elynn Cohen

Printed and bound in Korea

AUTHOR'S NOTE

STORIES of how the queen of Sheba challenged King Solomon with riddles and puzzles first appeared in the Talmud, a collection of Jewish laws and commentaries on the laws compiled between the early third and late fifth centuries. The Talmud also includes popular and instructive legends, parables, folklore, and wise sayings.

The renowned Jewish poet and author Hayyim Nahman Bialik (1873–1934) devoted a good part of his life to collecting, sorting, and rewriting Talmudic, other Jewish, and Arabic legends. He published them in several books, including *And It Came to Pass* (Hebrew Publishing Co., 1938), which is solely devoted to legends about King David and King Solomon.

My version of the following story is based on "The Bee," one of the stories in *And It Came to Pass*. That book's version mentions the interaction between the king and the bee, but since this account doesn't appear in the Talmud, scholars are unclear whether Bialik based it on some other ancient folklore or whether he invented it.

KING SOLOMON was the wisest and smartest king of his days. Not only could the king speak every language in the world, he could also talk to the animals.

The king lived in a big palace surrounded by a magnificent garden where beautiful flowers grew.

When it was hot in the palace, King Solomon was in the habit of taking his afternoon nap under the shade of a broad-leaf fig tree in his garden.

One day, while the king was sleeping under the tree, a young bee flew into the garden. It flew from one pretty flower to another, happily drinking the nectar. When it had had enough, the bee decided to rest and landed on, of all things, the king's nose.

This tickled the king. Half asleep, he raised his hand, the hand frightened the bee, and the bee stung the king's nose.

The pain woke King Solomon up. As his nose became swollen and the pain grew worse, his rage mounted. "What insect dared to sting the king's nose?" he shouted.

As his nose became redder and grew to be as big as a cucumber, he commanded with fury, "All bees, hornets, wasps, and flies, appear immediately before me!"

From every hive and nest, from near and far,
swarms of bees, hornets, wasps, and flies flew
in a panic to the king's garden.

They were all buzzing in confusion when King Solomon shouted, "Silence!" A hush fell upon all. Pointing to his nose, the king roared, "Who among you dared to do a thing like this to the king?" Nobody moved; nobody buzzed. "Who among you dared to do a thing like this to the king?" Solomon repeated.

Finally a small bee flew straight to him and said, "I am the one, my lord, my king." Before the king had time to get angry and punish the bee, it pleaded, "O my lord, my king, please don't be angry! I am a young and foolish bee. I have not yet learned the difference between a flower and a nose, or between one nose and another—especially the nose of my lord, my king, a nose with a roselike fragrance and a bananalike grace."

As the bee talked, a faint smile grew on King Solomon's face. The bee gathered more courage and continued, "I have sinned, my lord, my king, and I am sorry. Do not be angry with me; do not punish me. Who knows? Maybe one day, my lord, my king, I will be able to repay you with a favor."

King Solomon burst out laughing. "*You*, a little creature like you, will repay the king?" He laughed so much that he could not talk. He just motioned to the little bee and all the other insects to fly away.

When the king stopped laughing, his servant put ointment on his nose, and soon the pain and swelling went away.

Before long, the king forgot all about the bee.

One day the queen of Sheba came to the palace to visit King Solomon.

She had heard how smart the king was, and in order to test him, she had brought with her all sorts of difficult riddles, puzzles, and questions. One by one she presented them to the king, and one by one he solved them.

The time came for the last test.

The queen brought to the throne room several of her young maidens. Each of them held a bouquet of beautiful flowers. "Before you, O King Solomon, in the hands of the maidens, are bouquets of flowers. Only one of them is made up of real flowers. The rest of the flowers are made by human hands. Do, O king, tell me which is which!"

The man-made flowers looked so perfect, so much like flowers of the fields and gardens, that the king could not tell them apart. He looked and looked some more, and still could not tell them apart.

The king was ready to give up when he heard a faint buzz outside the window. He was the only one who heard it. When the king saw a little bee, his eyes lit up. "Open the window!" he told a servant. "Be quick!"

The window was opened. Without anybody else noticing, the bee flew in and headed straight for one bouquet. The king smiled and pointed at the bouquet where the bee settled.

"That is the bouquet of real flowers!" he exclaimed, to the amazement of the queen of Sheba and her maidens.

And that is how the little bee repaid the king.